the Nickle Nackle Tree

Lynley Dodd

PUFFIN BOOKS

1

In the Manglemunching Forest there's
a Nickle Nackle tree,
Growing Nickle Nackle berries that are
red as red can be.
I went to look last Monday; I was
too surprised for words
—On every twisty branch there was a
jumbly jam of birds.

One Ballyhoo bird, kicking up a din,

2

Two squawking Scritchet birds with
legs so twiggy thin.

3

Three Tittle Tattle birds with twirly curls behind,

4

Four lurking Yuk birds, the sly and
smirking kind.

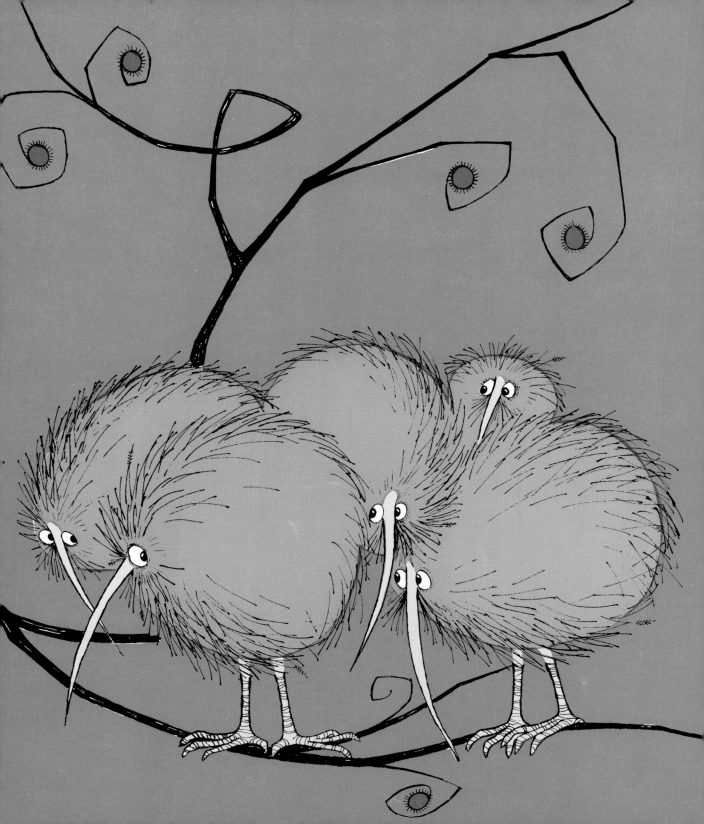

5

Five bashful Blush birds, trying
hard to hide,

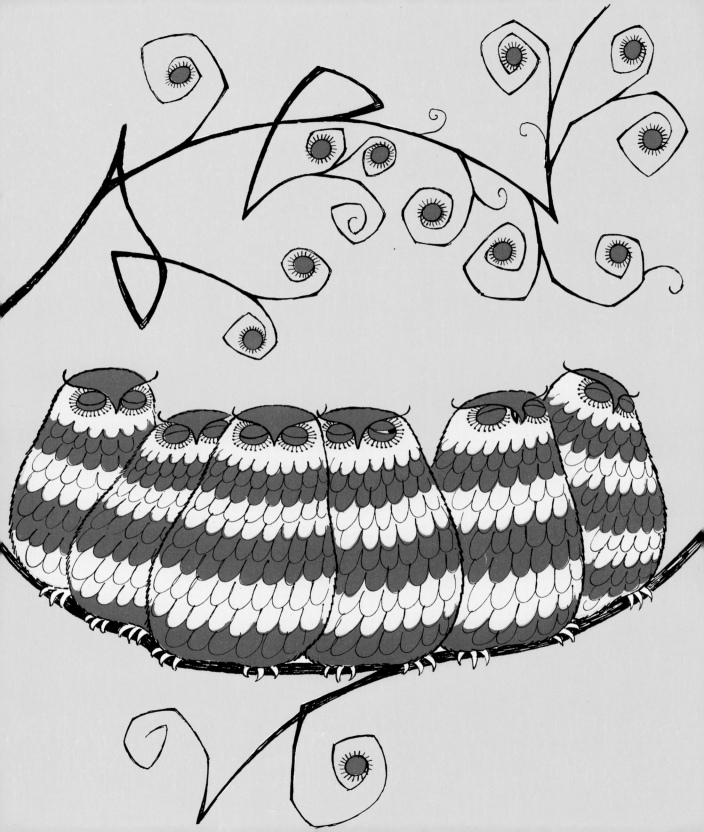

6

Six sleepy Snooze birds, snoring
side by side.

7

Seven haughty Huffpuff birds with
hoity-toity smiles,

8

Eight cheeky Chizzle birds in
cheerful chirpy piles.

9

Nine friendly Natter birds, building
nice new nests,

10

Ten fussy Fissick birds in yellow feathered vests.

11

Eleven singing Throstle birds with
rings around their eyes,

12

Twelve tiny Tweek birds—the very smallest size.

13

Thirteen grouchy Grudge birds,
grousing at the fun,

14

Fourteen pink Fandango birds,
dancing in the sun.

The tree was squeezed and jammed
and crammed as full as it could be . . .

I think it was an OVERLOADED
Nickle Nackle tree.